13086

Crocodiles

by Anne Welsbacher

Consultant:
The Staff of Black Hills Reptile Gardens
Rapid City, South Dakota

CAPSTONE
HIGH-INTEREST
BOOKS

an imprint of Capstone Press
Mankato, Minnesota

Capstone High-Interest Books are published by Capstone Press
151 Good Counsel Drive, P.O. Box 669, Mankato, Minnesota 56002
http://www.capstone-press.com

Library of Congress Cataloging-in-Publication Data
Welsbacher, Anne, 1955–
    Crocodiles/by Anne Welsbacher.
        p. cm.—(Predators in the wild)
    Includes bibliographical references (p. 31) and index.
    Summary: Describes the physical characteristics, hunting behavior, habitat, and
endangered status of crocodiles.
        ISBN 0-7368-1315-2
        1. Crocodiles—Juvenile literature. [1. Crocodiles. 2. Endangered species.]
I. Title. II. Series.
QL666.C925 W43 2003
597.98'2—dc21   2001007853

Editorial Credits
Carrie Braulick, editor; Karen Risch, product planning editor; Timothy Halldin,
    series designer; Gene Bentdahl, book designer and illustrator; Jo Miller,
    photo researcher

Photo Credits
Ann & Rob Simpson, 15, 17 (lower left, upper left)
Cheryl A. Ertelt, 17 (lower right)
Comstock, background elements
Daniel Gotshall/Visuals Unlimited, 24
Doug Perrine/Seapics.com, cover
Eye Ubiquitous/CORBIS, 28
Frank Cleland/Gnass Photo Images, 9, 20, 27
Frederick D. Atwood, 14, 17 (upper right)
Fritz Pölking/Visuals Unlimited, 18
Inga Spence/Visuals Unlimited, 16
James Beveridge/Visuals Unlimited, 8
James P. Rowan, 29
Joe McDonald, 21
Jonathan Blair/CORBIS, 10, 22
Jonathan Blair/Woodfin Camp & Associates, Inc., 11, 12
Tom & Pat Leeson, 6

1 2 3 4 5 6 07 06 05 04 03 02

Table of Contents

Common name:	Crocodile
Scientific name:	Crocodylus
Size:	Most crocodiles are 6 to 12 feet (1.8 to 3.7 meters) long. Some can grow up to 20 feet (6.1 meters) long.
Weight:	Crocodiles weigh between 20 and 1,700 pounds (9.1 and 771 kilograms).
Life span:	Scientists believe that crocodiles live between 30 and 50 years.
Habitat:	Crocodiles live in warm, wet regions. They live in swamps, marshes, lakes, ponds, and rivers. They may dig burrows in riverbanks or rest on land.

Prey: Crocodiles eat fish, birds, snakes, lizards, frogs, turtles, rats, antelope, and deer.

Abilities: Crocodiles are excellent swimmers. They can walk and run on land for short time periods. They also can crawl on their bellies to move across land.

Social Habits: Crocodiles share habitats with other crocodiles. They often communicate with each other. Male crocodiles defend their territories from other males during mating season.

In This Chapter:

* Crocodiles are the largest reptiles on Earth.

* Crocodiles have a thin snout and sharp teeth.

* Crocodiles are good swimmers.

Chapter 1

Crocodiles

Crocodiles are the largest reptiles in the world. Most crocodiles are 6 to 12 feet (1.8 to 3.7 meters) long. But some types of crocodiles can grow larger. The saltwater crocodile is the largest. It can grow to about 20 feet (6.1 meters) long. These crocodiles can weigh as much as 1,700 pounds (771 kilograms).

Crocodiles are closely related to dinosaurs. Both crocodiles and dinosaurs lived on Earth millions of years ago.

Species

Crocodiles belong to a reptile group called Crocodilia. Reptiles are cold-blooded. Their body temperature changes according to their surroundings. Other crocodilians include alligators, caimans, and gharials.

Scientists divide crocodiles into 14 species. Each species shares certain physical features.

Appearance

Like all crocodilians, crocodiles have short legs, long bodies, and long tails. Crocodiles have thin, pointed snouts. Their narrow eyes sit high on their heads. Crocodiles have about 60 sharp teeth.

Crocodiles are olive green to gray. Their belly usually is cream in color.

Scales cover a crocodile's body. The scales are made

Nests

Female crocodiles dig holes in the ground for their nests. They also may build mounds of plants and mud. Female crocodiles usually lay between 60 and 90 eggs in their nests. Females protect their nests from predators. Fish, birds, and other reptiles eat crocodile eggs.

Crocodiles have long bodies covered with scales.

of keratin. A person's fingernails also are made of this hard material. Some crocodiles have scales that form points on top of their backs. These scales are called scutes. Bony plates called osteoderms are underneath the scutes. They help warm crocodiles by absorbing heat from the sun.

Crocodiles can travel with their bellies above the ground.

Abilities

Crocodiles are good swimmers. They sweep their long tails from side to side to swim. They use their feet to steer.

Crocodiles can travel over land in various ways. They may crawl on their bellies to move over muddy areas. Crocodiles also can stretch their legs to lift their bellies above land. Crocodiles sometimes walk in this way over rough land or to step over objects.

Crocodiles can gallop to move quickly. They can gallop about 10 miles (16 kilometers) per hour. But they only can run at this speed for a few steps. Crocodiles sometimes gallop to escape danger.

Crocodiles can hold their breath for as long as one hour. This ability allows crocodiles to hunt or drown prey underwater. But crocodiles rarely stay underwater for more than 15 minutes.

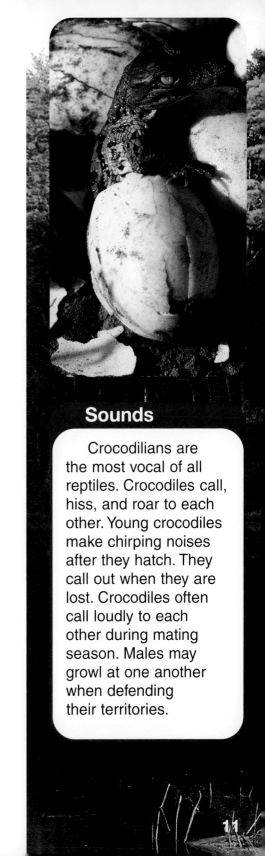

Sounds

Crocodilians are the most vocal of all reptiles. Crocodiles call, hiss, and roar to each other. Young crocodiles make chirping noises after they hatch. They call out when they are lost. Crocodiles often call loudly to each other during mating season. Males may growl at one another when defending their territories.

In This Chapter:

* Crocodiles are nocturnal.

* Crocodiles ambush their prey.

* Crocodiles catch prey in their strong jaws.

The Hunt

Crocodiles are carnivores. They eat meat from the animals that they hunt. In the water, crocodiles eat fish, frogs, and turtles. Crocodiles also hunt animals near the water. They eat birds, snakes, lizards, and rats. Crocodiles hunt large land animals that come to the water to drink. These animals include zebras, deer, and antelope. Crocodiles also eat carrion. They find this dead animal flesh in or near the water.

Staying Hidden

A crocodile waits for prey to come near. It hides with its body underwater so that prey does not

A crocodile keeps its eyes and nose above water as it floats.

notice it. Only the crocodile's eyes and nostrils
are visible.

A crocodile's camouflage coloring helps it
hide. Its green-gray colors blend in with mud
and plant matter on the water's surface.

Crocodiles stay hidden in other ways. They
are nocturnal. They hunt mainly at night or

near sundown. Crocodiles often lie still in slow-moving water. This water usually is cloudy and dirty. Prey cannot easily see crocodiles in the unclear water.

Ambushing Prey

A crocodile moves quickly toward prey to ambush it. The crocodile catches the animal in its strong jaws. A crocodile's jaws can produce a force of almost 12 tons (11 metric tons) as they clamp down on prey.

Crocodiles sometimes hunt land animals that come to the water to drink. They wait in shallow water near shore. Crocodiles use their jaws to grab an animal's snout or leg. They then can pull the animal into the water.

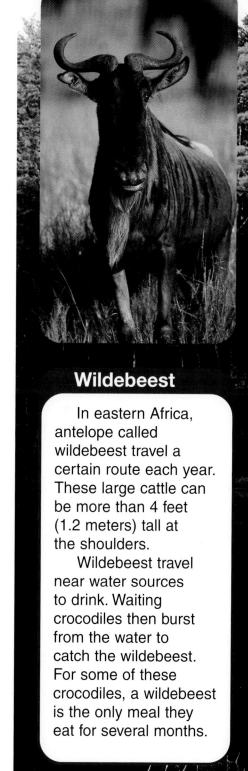

Wildebeest

In eastern Africa, antelope called wildebeest travel a certain route each year. These large cattle can be more than 4 feet (1.2 meters) tall at the shoulders.

Wildebeest travel near water sources to drink. Waiting crocodiles then burst from the water to catch the wildebeest. For some of these crocodiles, a wildebeest is the only meal they eat for several months.

Crocodiles use their vision to locate prey.

Hunting Senses

Crocodiles use mainly vision to locate prey. Crocodiles can see better than people can in low levels of light. The pupils in their eyes open wide to let in a great deal of light.

Crocodiles can keep their eyes open underwater. They have a third eyelid that moves sideways across the eye when crocodiles sink underwater. This clear eyelid protects the eye.

Crocodiles have a good sense of hearing. They can hear high-pitched sounds that people cannot hear.

What Crocodiles Eat

Waterbirds

Turtles

Fish

Wildebeest

In This Chapter:

* Crocodiles drown their prey.

* Crocodiles tear flesh from prey.

* Crocodiles eat every few weeks or months.

Chapter 3

The Kill

A crocodile often pulls prey underwater to drown it. A crocodile has a large flap of flesh at the back of its throat. This flap keeps water out of a crocodile's lungs as it drowns prey. A crocodile also can close its nostrils while underwater.

Crocodiles may use their jaws and teeth to crush prey. But they do not chew prey with their teeth. They must swallow food whole.

To swallow prey in water, a crocodile lifts its head out of the water. Muscles pull the flap at

the back of the throat down. The throat then opens and prey slides down the throat.

Large Prey

Large prey can be difficult for crocodiles to swallow whole. Crocodiles often spin and twist their bodies to tear off pieces of flesh from large prey. Groups of as many as 40 crocodiles sometimes join to eat large prey.

Few animals can fight off an adult crocodile. Adult crocodiles are large and strong. They have few

Crocodiles tear off pieces of flesh from large prey.

natural predators. But a crocodile that attacks a lion, tiger, or hippopotamus may be unable to kill it. These animals are strong enough to kill a crocodile.

Crocodiles usually swallow prey whole.

Digesting Food

A crocodile's digestive system is efficient. The
body uses almost all food that a crocodile
eats. Acids in a crocodile's stomach digest its
food. These acids are strong enough to break
down bones.

Crocodiles that eat a small meal may hunt
again soon. But crocodiles that eat a large meal
may go weeks or months without eating again.
Crocodiles can live up to one year without
eating. Their body fat can provide them with
energy for long periods of time.

Myth: Crocodiles move slowly.

Fact: Crocodiles can run about 10 miles (16 kilometers) per hour for short periods of time.

Myth: Crocodile attacks on people are common.

Fact: Crocodile attacks on people are rare. They are most common in areas where people often come into contact with crocodiles.

Myth: Crocodiles live for hundreds of years.

Fact: Scientists believe that crocodiles in the wild usually live 30 to 50 years. Some crocodiles in captivity have lived to be about 70 years old.

In This Chapter:

* Most crocodiles live in tropical waters.

* People killed many crocodiles in the past.

* Laws protect some crocodile species.

Chapter 4

In the World of People

Crocodiles live mainly in tropical regions around the world. These warm areas are located near the equator. This imaginary line circles the Earth at its center. It divides the Earth into northern and southern hemispheres. Most crocodiles live in South America, Africa, Asia, and Australia. They live in a variety of habitats such as swamps, marshes, and rivers.

Crocodile Attacks

Crocodiles sometimes attack people. Saltwater and Nile crocodiles are most likely to attack people. Other crocodiles usually ignore people.

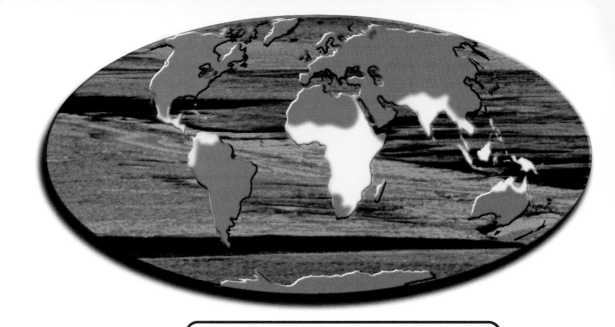

In some areas, crocodile attacks are rising. People take over crocodile habitats as they build roads and clear areas for farmland. The increased amount of contact between people and crocodiles makes attacks more common.

Threats to Crocodiles

Before the 1960s, many people hunted crocodiles for their skins. People used the skin to make leather purses, belts, and shoes. Other people destroyed crocodile habitats to create space for farmland or buildings. Some people killed crocodiles because they were afraid of them.

In many areas, crocodile populations declined. More than 2,000 American crocodiles had lived in Florida before the 1930s. But less than 200 remained by the 1970s.

Some scientists believe there once were thousands of Orinoco crocodiles living in Colombia and Venezuela. But between the 1930s and 1960s, many people hunted them and took over their habitat. Today, these crocodiles are endangered. Scientists believe they may die out soon.

Salt Water

Most crocodiles live in freshwater. This water contains little salt. Freshwater sources include ponds, lakes, marshes, and rivers. But saltwater crocodiles often live in salt water. The world's seas and oceans contain salt water. Saltwater crocodiles live near the coastal areas of southeastern Asia and northern Australia. They also live on islands between the coasts.

Ancient Beliefs

The ancient Egyptians worshiped many gods. They believed crocodiles represented a god named Sobek. They thought crocodiles were sacred animals. The ancient Egyptians placed gold ornaments on crocodiles. They preserved crocodiles' bodies after the reptiles died. They then placed the mummified bodies in tombs.

Crocodile Survival

During the 1970s, many governments throughout the world passed laws to protect crocodiles. In 1973, an international meeting outlawed the trade of crocodile skins for endangered species and species with declining populations. The U.S. government passed the Endangered Species Act in 1973. This law protects animals listed as endangered. Government officials soon added American crocodiles to this list.

Some people have formed groups to protect crocodiles. The Crocodile Specialist Group studies crocodiles and develops plans to protect crocodile habitats.

Some crocodiles live in protected areas.

People also establish crocodile farms. Workers at these farms keep eggs safe from predators. They then release young crocodiles into the wild.

Scientists keep track of crocodile populations. They hope that people will continue to help crocodiles survive in the future.

Words to Know

ambush (AM-bush)—to hide and then attack

camouflage (KAM-uh-flahzh)—coloring or covering that makes animals, people, and objects look like their surroundings

carnivore (KAR-nuh-vohr)—an animal that eats meat

carrion (KARE-ee-uhn)—dead animal flesh

Crocodilia (krah-kuh-DIH-lee-uh)—a reptile group that includes crocodiles, alligators, caimans, and gharials

digest (dye-JEST)—to break down food so that it can be used by the body

endangered species (en-DAYN-jured SPEE-sheez)—a type of animal that is in danger of dying out

nocturnal (nok-TUR-nuhl)—active at night

reptile (REP-tile)—a cold-blooded animal with a backbone

To Learn More

Dudley, Karen. *Alligators and Crocodiles.* The Untamed World. Austin, Texas: Raintree Steck-Vaughn, 1998.

Jango-Cohen, Judith. *Crocodiles.* Animalways. New York: Benchmark Books, 2001.

Simon, Seymour. *Crocodiles and Alligators.* New York: HarperCollins Publishers, 1999.

Woodward, John. *Crocodiles and Alligators.* Endangered! New York: Benchmark Books, 1999.

Useful Addresses

Black Hills Reptile Gardens
P.O. Box 620
Rapid City, SD 57709

Rainforest Reptile Refuge Society
1395-176 Street
Surrey, BC V3S 9S7
Canada

Society for the Study of Amphibians and Reptiles
Department of Biology
St. Louis University
3507 Laclede Avenue
St. Louis, MO 63103-2010

Internet Sites

The Crocodile Files
http://www.oneworldmagazine.org/tales/crocs/
  index.html

**Crocodilians: Natural History and
  Conservation**
http://www.crocodilian.com

Discovery.com—Crocodiles
http://www.discovery.com/stories/nature/crocs/
  tour.html

Index